Rumpelstiltskin RETURNS

By Maggie Pearson

Illustrated by Steve Stone

Crabtree Publishing Company
www.crabtreebooks.com

Crabtree Publishing Company
www.crabtreebooks.com
1-800-387-7650

616 Welland Ave.
St. Catharines, ON
L2M 5V6

PMB 59051, 350 Fifth Ave.
59th Floor,
New York, NY 10118

Published by Crabtree Publishing Company in 2015

First published in 2012 by Franklin Watts
(A division of Hachette Children's Books)

Text © Maggie Pearson 2012
Illustration © Steve Stone 2012

Series editor: Melanie Palmer
Series advisor: Catherine Glavina
Series designer: Peter Scoulding
Editor: Kathy Middleton
**Proofreader and
   notes to adults:** Shannon Welbourn
**Production coordinator and
   Prepress technician:** Margaret Amy Salter
Print coordinator: Katherine Berti

Printed in Hong Kong/082014/BK20140613

**Library and Archives Canada
Cataloguing in Publication**

CIP is available at the Library and Archives Canada

**Library of Congress
Cataloging-in-Publication Data**

Pearson, Maggie, 1941-
 Rumpelstiltskin returns / by Maggie Pearson ;
illustrated by Steve Stone.
     pages cm. -- (Race ahead with reading)
 "First published in 2012 by Franklin Watts"--
Copyright page.
  ISBN 978-0-7787-1332-6 (reinforced library
binding) -- ISBN 978-0-7787-1333-3 (pbk.) --
ISBN 978-1-4271-7779-7 (electronic pdf) --
ISBN 978-1-4271-7767-4 (electronic html)
 [1. Characters in literature--Fiction. 2. Magic--
Fiction.] I. Stone, Steve, 1974- illustrator. II. Title.

 PZ7.P32315Ru 2014
 [E]--dc23
                                    2014020440

Chapter One

As I was walking home from school one day, I heard a voice calling, "Help me!"

I looked around.

There was no one there.

"Help me!" the voice cried.

"Help! This big stone is on top of me!"

I looked down and saw the big stone.
Then I saw a little brown shoe
sticking out from under it.

So I rolled that big stone out of the way.
Out popped a funny little man. He looked
like his arms and legs had been made out
of sticks, and his hair was like yellow
cotton candy.

"You've helped old Rumpelstiltskin,"
the little man said. "Now it's
my turn to help you."
"Help me?" I said. "How?"

"Any way you want! I'm your servant now.
When you've got work to do, I'll do it for
you. From now on you can just have fun."

"What about my mom?" I said. I really wasn't sure what she would say about Rumpelstiltskin moving in with us.

"She won't even see me," he said. "Nobody will. It will be our secret."

"All right," I said. "It's a deal!"

"Just don't ever thank me. I hate it if people say thank you!" Rumpelstiltskin said.

Then, in a flash of light, he was gone.

Chapter Two

"Clean your room!" Mom called out as I went up the stairs.

I smiled to myself. Time to call on Rumpelstiltskin.

But Rumpelstiltskin had already got there ahead of me. Everything was so neat and tidy, it didn't look like my room at all.

I got out my homework. Today it was math. I'm terrible at math. But Rumpelstiltskin had done it for me!

The next day at school, I got ten out of ten on my homework. But the teacher didn't think I had done it all by myself. I had to stay in at recess and do it all over again, so she could watch me do it. Luckily, I still got the answers right!

After school we played soccer. I'm usually no good at soccer. That day I scored goal after goal.

GOAL

GOAL

No one could get the ball away from me.
Whenever I aimed for the goal, the ball
went in.

GOAL!

GOAL!

I knew it was Rumpelstiltskin
doing it. But nobody else
could see him.

In the end everyone got fed up and went home. I was angry, so I shouted out, "Rumpelstiltskin! I want a word with you! When I want your help, I'll ask for it."

"No need to ask," he said.
"I do all the work.
You have all the fun.
That was our deal."

"Soccer is fun!" I said.

"It looked more like hard work to me," he replied.

Chapter Three

Every day Rumpelstiltskin made my bed
and cleaned my shoes.

He tidied my room up,
and he did my homework.

16

He weeded the garden
and mowed the lawn.

He did the dishes for Dad.

He washed the
car for Mom.

My parents thought I was doing it all. They told all their friends about me. And I was at the top of the class.

But nobody likes a show-off. I was the teacher's pet, and I was losing all my friends.

"Rumpelstiltskin!" I yelled. "I don't want you to be my servant any more."

"You said I could be your servant if I wanted to," he said. "And I do. I want to be your servant forever!"

But I didn't want Rumpelstiltskin to be my servant forever and ever. What could I do?

Chapter Four

There had to be something I could do by myself—something Rumpelstiltskin couldn't help me do. Maybe then he'd leave me alone.

I thought about it.
I thought and thought.

One day, I had an idea! I entered a summer fun run. I'm a rotten runner. I knew I couldn't win. And Rumpelstiltskin couldn't make me.

He'd have to pick me up and carry me if he wanted me to win. Then people would see him. I didn't think he wanted that.

Chapter Five

The day of the race came.

The starter raised his pistol.

Ready, set—GO!

Two of the runners tripped over their own feet. Someone had tied their laces together——guess who!

Then two runners started fighting.
Each one said the other had punched him
in the ribs. I knew who it really was.

Another was stung by
a wasp and had to go
to the first aid tent.
This didn't look good.

I set off with the rest of the runners, following the signs down the path and into the woods.

I passed runners who had lost a shoe in the mud, and others who had sprained their ankles or tripped and scraped their knees.

I saw signs swing around to point in the wrong direction, then swing back for me after the runners ahead had gone the wrong way.

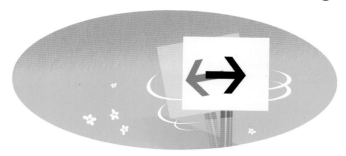

In the end I stopped and sat down.

"Rumpelstiltskin!" I yelled.
"I'm not moving until you promise
to let me finish this race by myself.
No more tricks! I can do this on my own,
thanks very much. I don't need any help
from you."

"What did you say?" asked Rumpelstiltskin.
"You said, 'Thanks very much.' Didn't I
tell you not to thank me?" he yelled.
"If there's one thing I can't stand it's
people thanking me!"

He stamped his foot.
"I won't be thanked!
I won't! I won't!
You'll get no more help
from Rumpelstiltskin!"

He started spinning around and around.
"You can tidy your own room and do
your own homework!" he yelled.
He was spinning so fast now,
he was just a blur.

Then, in a flash, he was gone.

I could still hear him shouting,

"You'll never see Rumpelstiltskin again!"

"Thanks very much!" I yelled back,

just to make sure that I never did.

Notes for Adults

These entertaining, first chapter books help children build up their reading skills so they can move on to longer books. Fun illustrations and bite-sized chapters encourage young readers to take the driver's seat and *Race Ahead with Reading.*

THE FOLLOWING BEFORE, DURING, AND AFTER READING ACTIVITY SUGGESTIONS SUPPORT LITERACY SKILL DEVELOPMENT AND CAN ENRICH SHARED READING EXPERIENCES:

BEFORE

1. Make reading fun! Choose a time to read when you and the reader are relaxed and have time to share the story together. Don't forget to give praise! Children learn best in a positive environment.
2. Before reading, ask the reader to look at the title and illustration on the cover of the book **Rumpelstiltskin Returns**. Invite them to make predictions about what will happen in the story. They may make use of prior knowledge and make connections to other stories they have heard or read about Rumpelstiltskin or another character that grants wishes.

DURING

3. Encourage readers to determine unfamiliar words themselves by using clues from the text and illustrations.
4. During reading, encourage the child to review his or her understanding and see if they want to revise their predictions midway. Encourage the reader to make text-to-text connections, choosing a part of the story that reminds them of another story they have read; and text-to-self connections, choosing a part of the story that relates to their own personal experiences; and text-to-world connections, choosing a part of the story that reminds them of something that happened in the real world.

AFTER

5. Ask the reader **who** the main characters are in this story. Have the child retell the story in their own words. Ask him or her to think about the predictions they made before reading the story. How were they the same or different?

DISCUSSION QUESTIONS FOR KIDS

6. Throughout this story, the girl is presented with problems. How does she solve the problems she faces?
7. How did the girl's new-found success affect her relationships with friends and family?
8. Rumpelstiltskin tells the girl to keep him a secret from her parents. What would you do? What choices would you make?
9. Have you ever felt sorry about something you did? Was it about a decision that you made? Was it a good or bad decision? Explain why.
10. If you could have someone help make you better at something what would it be and why?
11. Create your own story or drawing about a problem or challenge you had and how you solved it.